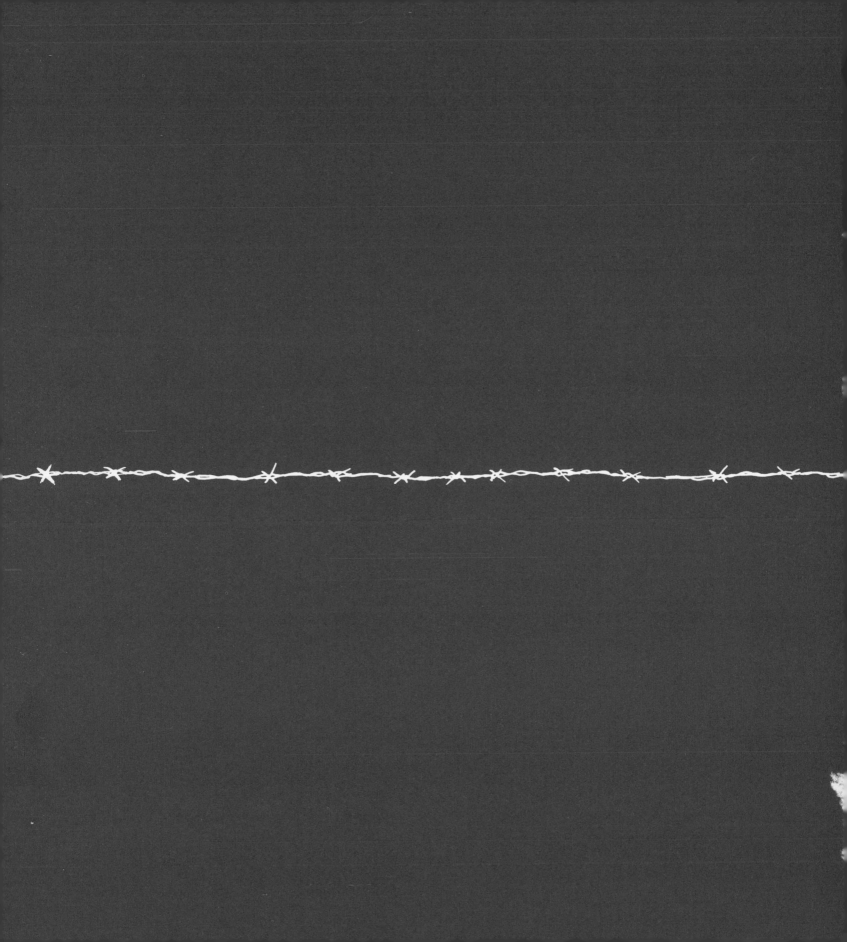

a child's garden

a child's garden

a story of hope

michael foreman

CANDLEWICK PRESS

The boy saw it after a night of rain,
a speck of green in the rubble, peeping up toward the sunlight.
He moved some broken bricks so that nothing would fall and
crush the tiny plant. He didn't know what sort of plant it was, a
flower or a weed; he just knew it would have to struggle to survive.

The boy searched around and found an old can that
held a little rainwater. He brought it to the plant.

"Drink up," he whispered. "Drink up."

The sun was climbing in the sky, and the boy gave the
plant shade with some old sacking and wire.

The boy's world was a place of ruin and rubble, ringed by a fence of barbed wire. In the hot, dry summer, the air was thick with dust. Faraway hills shimmered in the haze. The boy knew that cool streams flowed in those hills. He had once gone there with his father, but now the hills were on the wrong side of the wire.

Over the following weeks, he cared for his secret garden. Soon the green tendrils reached to the high barbed-wire fence. Now the boy could tell it was a vine—a grapevine.

It spread along the fence and gave shade to its own tender roots, which in turn sent out more shoots.

Birds and butterflies came, bringing seeds and pollen on their wings. The garden grew. It was no longer a secret.

Friends came to sit in its shade,

and it became a playground for the children.

Then, one day, soldiers came
and destroyed everything.
They threw the vine in
a ditch on the other
side of the wire.

The boy thought his heart would break.

Winter came.

The boy and his family shivered in the cold and damp of their ruined home.

Spring came late. After the first night of rain for weeks, the boy noticed green shoots all along the ditch. Some seeds from his vine must have survived the winter. He worried about the new shoots. He couldn't get close enough to water them. They were on the other side of the wire.

Then, one evening, he saw a little girl playing by the ditch.

She had a bucket, and she was sprinkling water on the tiny plants.

Each evening she returned.
The boy hoped the soldiers wouldn't notice. But they
didn't seem to mind plants growing on their side of the fence.

Before long, the boy saw tiny specks of green peeping from the rubble where his garden had been.

"Look!" he yelled. "Come and see! My vine has come back!"

He began collecting water and once more tended his garden.
Soon it reached the wire, where it became entwined with
the green tendrils from the little girl's side.

The barbed wire disappeared under leafy shade, and the new garden became home once more to birds and butterflies.

Let the soldiers return, thought the boy.

Roots are deep, and seeds spread....

One day the fence will disappear forever,

and we will be able to walk again into the hills.

To my friend Dr. Martin Bax,
who has improved the lives of so many
children around the world

First U.S. edition 2009

Library of Congress Cataloging-in-Publication Data is available.

Library of Congress Catalog Card Number 2008935656

ISBN 978-0-7636-4271-6

2 4 6 8 10 9 7 5 3 1

Printed in China

This book was typeset in Historical FellType.
The illustrations were done in pencil and watercolor.

Candlewick Press
99 Dover Street
Somerville, Massachusetts 02144

visit us at www.candlewick.com